Enjoy!
David B. Brin
(and Herman 🐾!)

The Discontented Rabbit

David A. Rives & Tom Newsom

Moon River Publishing
812 Natchez Avenue
Liberty, MO 64068
Phone: (800) 522-7735
Email: davidrives@hotmail.com
Website: www.MoonRiverPublishing.com

ISBN: 978-1-878143-04-4

1 2 3 4 5 6 7 8 9 10

This book is dedicated to

Robert J. Finkel, Esq.

of

Detroit, Michigan,

whose generosity made it possible

There once was a rabbit named Herman, who had very big ears.
Yes, we know: _all_ rabbits have very big ears. But Herman's were...

...EXCEPTIONALLY big!

And not only that, but they seemed to have a mind of their own: Sometimes, and with no warning, they'd just stick straight up, so Herman couldn't get into his house!

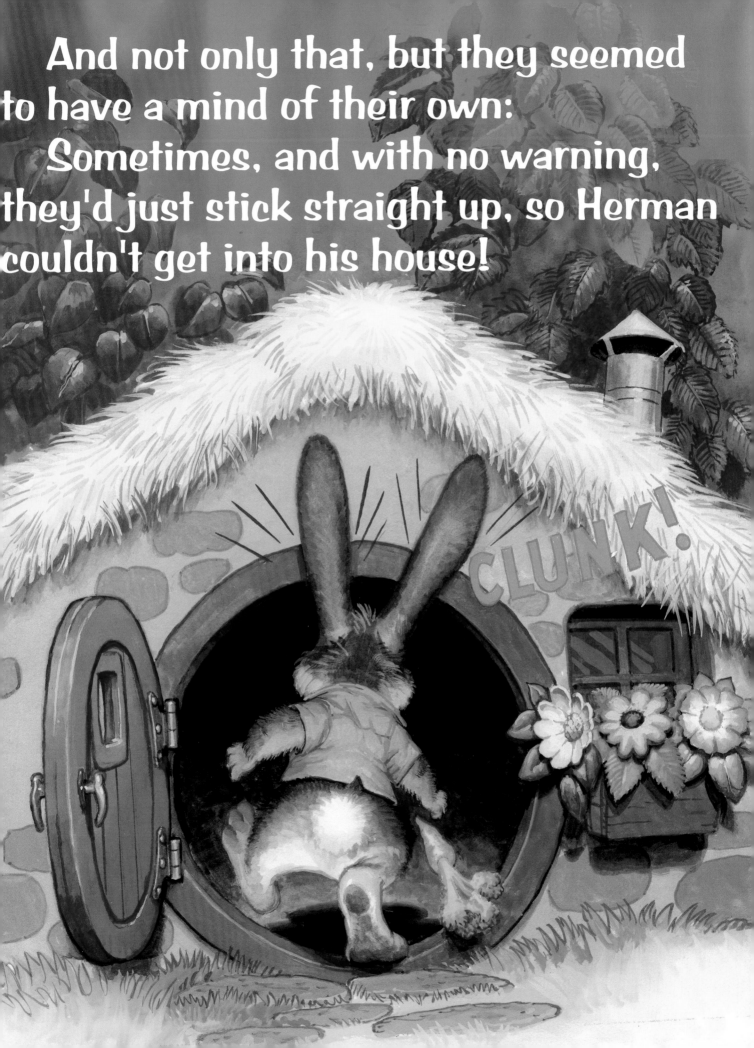

CLUNK!

And other times they'd droop, and get into his soup!

Or his brothers and sisters, with time on their hands, would sneak up on Herman when he was asleep...

...and tie his ears in
all sorts of knots!

And when his Mother's backyard clothesline got full...

Finally, Herman had had enough. "I hate my ears!" he cried, and vowed, right then and there, to do something about them!

His first stop was at a plastic surgeon's, to see if the nice man could make Herman's ears smaller.

"Of course I can," the surgeon said. "And here's what it'll cost you."

Herman couldn't _remember_ the last time he'd moved that fast!

Then one day, when he was picking stickers out of his ears, Herman got the idea of a lifetime:

"I know," he said, "I'll just *trade* my ears for *somebody else's!*"

So, off to the library Herman went, to see whose ears he could possibly trade for.

Well, it didn't take long for Herman to realize that the place with the most animals in the world had to be Africa, so that's where he knew he had to go.

His next stop, by the river's edge, was a lot more promising.

"Can I help you?" the hippopotamus asked.

"Yes. My name is Herman and I hate my ears, so I'd like to trade them for yours."

"Mm-hm. And why would I want your ears instead of mine?"

"Well, you can twirl your ears around, right?"

"That's right."

"Well, if you had my ears, then, when you twirled them around, you could scratch your neck at the same time..."

"...or wipe the sleep out of your eyes..."

"...or dab the corners of your mouth after you've eaten."

"I see. Well, that sounds like it would be a very good trade for me--"
   Now Herman was getting excited!
"--but you're forgetting one thing:"
"What's that?"
"I spend most of my life underwater."

"So?"

"So, sound travels much *faster* underwater than it does in the air, and it's much, much *louder*."

"So?"

"So, I don't need to have very good hearing, to know when an alligator has slipped into the water and started coming after me. That's why my ears can be so small.

"You, on the other hand, need very _good_ hearing, to know when a coyote's decided he'd like you for lunch!"

"So I'm afraid my ears wouldn't do you much good."

"Hmph!" Herman said, trying very hard to hide his disappointment.

"I know: Why don't you try Izzy, the impala? His ears aren't very big, and they can hear a lion from a mile away. He lives on the other side of that hill over there."

Herman looked where the hippo was pointing.

"Thanks," he said, and started off toward the hill.

Izzy was in his front yard, eating his garden, when Herman arrived.

The much-taller animal looked up from the radishes.

"Can I help you?"

"Yes. My name is Herman, and I hate my ears, so I'd like to trade them for yours."

"I see. And why would I want your ears instead of mine?"

"Well, for one, you could flop them over your eyes at night, to help you get to sleep."

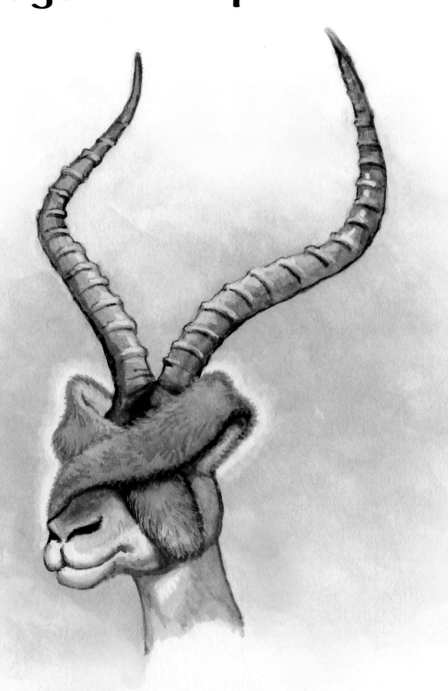

"Or you could wave them around, when a lion was coming, to warn all the other impalas."

"Or you could use them as a weather vane, to see which way the wind was blowing, so you could always be _downwind_ from the lions."

"Mm-hm. Well, that all sounds very good--"
Again Herman was getting excited.
"--except for one thing:"
Oh no, Herman thought, *not again.*
"What if your ears kept getting caught on my horns? Then they couldn't do any of the wonderful things you say they can do."

Herman thought about that for a moment; thought about his ears keeping him out of his house when they suddenly decided to spring straight up. But that only happened once in a blue moon.

If he took the impala's _horns_, however, along with his ears, he'd _never_ get back in his house; he'd be stuck outside _forever_!

"So, what do you say, little rabbit?"

"Uh, can I get back to you on that?" which the impala knew the rabbit would never do.

"You know," Izzy said, "you might try the lions."

"EXCUSE ME?!"

"Yes, I know. But when they're not hungry, they can be quite charming."

"Well-l-l-l..."

"The nearest pride lives just on the other side of that forest over there. If you're lucky..."

Herman still wasn't convinced, but he thanked the impala and hopped off toward the forest.

When he got to the other side, he crept slowly through the tall brush, up to the big cat.

"Psst!"

The lioness raised her head. "Yes?"

"Are you hungry?"

"No, we just ate."

"Good."

Herman hopped out of the brush.

"And what can I do for you?"

"Well, my name is Herman, and I hate my ears, so I'd like to trade them for yours."

"I see. And why would I want to do that?"

"Well, for one, instead of carrying your babies around in your mouth all the time, you could make a little car seat for them, and tote them around on the back of your neck."

"That way, you wouldn't keep getting all that baby fur in your mouth."

"So, what do you say?"

"Well, that all sounds very good. But you're forgetting one thing:"

"What's that?"

"The minute your friends and family catch sight of my ears, they'll head for the hills like they've been shot out of a cannon! You'll never _see_ them again!"

"So, I'd be more than happy to give you your trade, but..."

Herman stopped for a moment and thought about that; thought about being all alone in the world, forever and ever.

"Uh...no thanks."

"You know, you might have better luck with the rhinoceros. He lives just down the road a piece."

So, off Herman went.

RHINOCEROS —A PIECE—

"Can I help you?" the rhinoceros asked.

"Yes. My name is Herman, and I hate my ears, so I'd like to trade them for yours."

"Oh, thank goodness!" the rhinoceros said. "I've been _waiting_ for someone to trade me their ears!"

"You have?!"

"Oh, absolutely! You see, hunters are always after me, for my wonderful horns.

"And even when I hide behind a bush, hoping they won't see me, my ears still stick up, so they know I'm there."

"If I had _your_ ears, they'd think I was a rabbit, and they'd leave me alone. So, here..."

The rhinoceros started taking off his ears, to trade them for Herman's, but all Herman could think of was...

"Uh, can I get back to you on that?"
"But you just said--"
But Herman was GONE!!!

When he was far enough down the road, Herman pulled out his list and went over it again. Then he lifted his head.

"This is unbelievable!" he said. "I've got ears that can help a person get to sleep at night, then help him wake up in the morning; that can scratch his neck when it itches or dab his mouth after he's eaten; that can warn the other animals when danger is near, or tell them which way the wind is blowing, so they can stay out of harm's way altogether; that can help them carry their babies around the way babies _should_ be carried!

"I've got ears that can do all that and I can't get anyone to _trade_ me for them? Or at least make a trade that won't get me _killed_, or lose me all my _friends_?!"

At which point, Herman stopped dead in his tracks, and thought about what he'd just said.

"Wait a minute: I've got ears that can do all that and I'm trying to get _rid_ of them?! Holy cow: what was I thinking?!"

And it was at that very moment that Herman _stopped_ hating his ears and started _loving_ them instead.

"Yes," he thought, "they can be a pain in the cottontail sometimes, but so can everything else on this goofy little planet.

"So, if I have to take a bit of the bad to get gobs of the good, then that's exactly what I'm going to do, from now on!"

And that's exactly what Herman did do -- from that day and forevermore.